Other Books by Tony Seton

Long Short Fiction Truth

The Larger Reality / The Realm of Higher Consciousness

Do You Mind?

The Ultimate App

Covid Blue

Thought So

True Tens / Seven Women of Beautiful Character

Say It Write

Dead as a Doorbell

The Bright Wise Solution

Is There a Why?

13 Days of Fear

Selected Writings

Deki-san

Equinox

Mokki's Peak

No Soap, Radio

Paradise Pond

Silent Alarm

The Autobiography of John Dough, Gigolo

Silver Lining

The Omega Crystal/New Moves

Truth Be Told

Mayhem

Jennifer

The Francie LeVillard Mysteries - Volumes I-XI

The Francie LeVillard Mysteries - The Early Years

Just Imagine

Trinidad Head

Musings on Sherlock Holmes

The Brink

The Quality Interview / Getting It Right
    on Both Sides of the Mic

From Terror to Triumph /
    The Herma Smith Curtis Story

Don't Mess with the Press / How to Write,
    Produce, and Report Quality Television News

Right Car, Right Price

The Flight of KAL 007

The Flight of KAL 007

An original screenplay by
Tony Seton

Carmel, California

February 2025

The Flight of KAL 007

ISBN 13: 978-0-9989605-6-2

Printed in the United States of America

Author's Note

This screenplay was originally written in 1984, the year after Korean Airlines flight 007 was mistaken for an American spy plane and shot down by a Soviet fighter plane.

In 2017, I pulled it out of a musty folder in the back of a file cabinet, blew off some dust, and read it. I found it to be sadly contemporary 30-some years later.

Governments around the world are spending over two trillion dollars a year on things military, with the United States paying 39% of the total, more than the next ten squanderers combined.

Of course ultimately our future will not be determined by who has the most lethal weapons. It will be how we can defuse the primitive thinking that deems them necessary.

The race is on. Not of arms but of hearts and minds.

Tony Seton
Carmel, California
November 2021

The Players

David STONE - Network television correspondent

MARGE Stone - David's wife

Benton JENNINGS - High-level CIA executive

Constance CHANEY - Washington fashion model

Pentagon CAPTAIN - sedentary, slow

Pentagon LT. COLONEL - Black, West Point erect.

CONGRESSMAN - squeaky clean, young intense

Norbert FOUNTS - President's CoS; short, stocky

Ed REIMER - President's Chief Foreign Policy Advisor; aristocratic tall and thin

HOSTESS

General KRUTZOFF - Sakhalin Security Chief; large, worn

Colonel POKOV- Deputy Security Chief at Sakhalin; hatchet face

Major Anton ILLUVYCH - Mig-23 fighter pilot; rugged

Harry DAMON - STONE's bureau chief; clever

Secretary of STATE

PRESIDENT

SOVIET PREMIER

US Destroyer COMMANDER

STEWARDESS

PILOT

CO-PILOT

NAVIGATOR

Soviet CONTROL PRESIDENT

Krutzoff's AIDE (Lieutenant)

PRESS SECRETARY

SOVIET COMMANDER

White House SECRETARY

OFFICER HOSTESS

TELEVISION COMMENTATOR

CIA DEPUTY

PREMIER

Congressman's ASSISTANT (Fred)

President's VALET

US Destroyer EXEC

The Flight of KAL 007

SCENE I - MARGE and David STONE are lying on the beach looking at the stars. The beach is deserted, the waves gentle, lighted only by the moon and stars.

MARGE

I am so glad that you finally agreed to take a week off. (Nestling closer) They have been running you ragged for thirteen weeks.

STONE

(Sighs) I'm glad it's over, too. But I think it was worthwhile. I know they liked my work, especially when I was covering the State Department during the Begin resignation. (He closes his eyes to push the images away.)

MARGE

You did an excellent job, darling, but is

there anyone at the network who appreci-
ates your work who's not afraid of you?
Seriously. (She raises her voice over his
protest.) You should be covering the White
House. You know what's going on better
than most of those turkeys.

STONE

This is true. (With mock concern) Do you
think we should go back?

MARGE

(Smiling lasciviously, begins to nibble on
his ear) Well, we can if you want, but you
know that if we go back, whatever story is
going to break, will wait for you to leave
again. That's what happened during our
honeymoon if you'll remember. We post-
poned it for five months so you wouldn't
have to leave the Watergate story, and
when we finally did take a week off, Dean
was fired, and Haldeman, Ehrlichman, and
Kleindienst all resigned.

STONE

(Wondering, musing, then lightening up) I

suppose you're right. But what if I start going through journalistic withdrawal?

MARGE

(She pushes him down on the sand, kissing him passionately; then she pulls away.) If you get bored, I brought the little TV; you can probably pick up something, even out here in the sticks.

STONE

I'll let you know if I get bored.

He pulls her down to him gently, and they embrace. As her head moves down, the moon is revealed directly in the camera angle.

SCENE II - The shot dissolves to the sun shining fractally through the leaves of a humid summer morning as the camera moves along slightly behind two runners jogging by the Jefferson Memorial. Benton JENNINGS's ambition to look ten years younger than his forty-six years can't compete with the heat. Constance CHANEY could pass for under thirty but for the experience in her eyes. Her running is effortless; she would not insult her friend by slowing her pace.

CHANEY

We've had this conversation before, Ben, but I have to tell you that I think you are pushing too hard. I think they see that you're pushing too hard, and that's why they're not promoting you faster. (SHE watches his face as the truth briefly creases it.) But you can't really complain. You are in the top management stratum of the CIA. That's not bad for someone your age, with your lack of political experience.

JENNINGS

(Turning his head sharply; he knows what she means.) I don't know why you keep bringing that up, Chaney. Just because I didn't pay dues in the '76 campaign doesn't mean that I didn't work hard enough in '80. And besides, I understand global politics better than anyone at Langley.

HE turns off into a park, runs a few yards and drops into the grass. SHE starts stretching on the sit-ups bench.

CHANEY

No doubt, my love, and maybe if they'd listen to you, we wouldn't have had to start up the Cold War again.

JENNINGS

(Looking at her quizzically) I don't know. The Russians have certainly been in there raising the ante. Look how they took advantage of that idiot Ford. And Carter! (HE stretches. When he begins again, he is forcing his voice to be even.) You know they're testing the new SS-30 on Wednesday night?

CHANEY

(Genuine disappointment on her face) Why? Why do they keep building? Who are they going to be able to kill faster? (Her voice is rising, the words coming in bursts between sit-ups.) When are they going to stop? (She finishes the sit-ups and turns on him accusingly, her voice suddenly quiet.) And when are we going to stop?

They look at each other for several long seconds. It is an old argument, repeated in hopes of getting some sudden understanding from the other. CHANEY stoops in front of JENNINGS, resting her hands on his knee.

CHANEY

(Looking down into his face) I don't have an assignment until 10. And we're only ten minutes from your apartment...

JENNINGS

(Relaxes, smiles) Let's go. (They start running.)

CHANEY

Is this new missile in violation of one of the SALT agreements?

JENNINGS

Yes, but the Senate decided not to ratify.

CHANEY

(Softly) One for our side.

JENNINGS

They're not going to get away with it this time.

The steely tone of his voice pulls at something inside of CHANEY and SHE trips but quickly regains her balance.

CHANEY

What does that mean?

JENNINGS

(He runs, continuing to look ahead, making her wait, watching her out of the corner of his eye.) This time, we're going to have proof.

They turn a corner, run past a black Mercedes convertible with the license plate "BENTON 1" and bound up the steps of a brownstone. The front door closes.

SCENE III - The shower door opens as JENNINGS joins CHANEY under the spray. There is soap in his eyes, so he does not see the startled look on her face when he speaks.

JENNINGS

I'm going to take a few days off and go backpacking at Shenandoah. Leaving tomorrow morning.

He ducks his head into the spray and the bubbles fly all over the camera's lens. The shot dissolves to

SCENE IV - Sakhalin Air Base, and the billowing parachute behind a MiG-23 that has just landed. The plane taxies to the hangar. Out of the cockpit, Major ILLUVYCH looks around at the barren, colorless scenery before stepping down the ladder. He salutes the waiting mechanics, they say something, and point him in the direction of the operations building. He makes some remark about their taking care of his things in the plane and walks off. His face shows fatigue, and he is not happy about the surroundings.

SCENE V - HE enters the operations building and is directed by the DESK OFFICER up the stairs. He finds the door open to the office of the security chief. From inside, he can hear pounding on a file cabinet.

SCENE VI - As HE enters, he sees KRUTZOFF, the security chief, and his AIDE. They are struggling to get a file drawer back in the cabinet. ILLUVYCH simply stands and watches. KRUTZOFF sees the major, steps back, leaving the file drawer in the straining arms of his AIDE.

KRUTZOFF

The major looks as though he is well versed in how the State intended file drawers to fit in their cabinets.

ILLUVYCH snaps to attention.

ILLUVYCH

Air Major Anton Illuvych, at your service, General.

ILLUVYCH puts his coat carefully over the back of a chair, walks over to the AIDE, lifts the drawer out of his arms and slips it into the cabinet, sliding it back and forth to make sure that it is on the rollers correctly.

The AIDE scowls, and leaves after an impatient nod from KRUTZOFF, closing the door behind him.

KRUTZOFF moves behind his desk, rummages through the papers for a moment, and draws out a file. HE squints at it, and finds and puts on his glasses. He gestures for ILLUVYCH to be seated in a chair before the desk.

KRUTZOFF

So, Major, it seems that you thought your unit could make it without you for two weeks while your wife had a baby.

ILLUVYCH

(Not being sure of the man; slipping into a safe pattern) Yes, Comrade General, the State generously allowed me two extra weeks in Tbilisi to be with her. It is our first child.

KRUTZOFF

Yes, (musing) the State is so generous. And now here you are, in the middle of no-where. Do you know during the winter, this is considered the worst post in the command? That's almost six months.

POKOV

(He has entered unseen, but strutting. When he speaks, ILLUVYCH doesn't turn but sees the mixture of fear and contempt on KRUTZOFF's face.) But one of the most vital in military terms, nonetheless, General.

KRUTZOFF

Colonel Pokov, Major Illuvych. (ILLUVYCH now stands and shakes hands with POKOV.) The major is the final member of our new green squadron. Colonel Pokov...

POKOV

I know all about the major; his is a distinguished record, for someone who's never seen real combat.

KRUTZOFF

Colonel Pokov is my assistant. (He stresses the title.)

KRUTZOFF and POKOV shake hands stiffly. There is a curious silence, finally broken when POKOV looks pointedly from KRUTZOFF to a "classified" folder he brought into the room with him.

KRUTZOFF

(To ILLUVYCH, nodding to the door) Tell the lieutenant to put you in the married officers' quarters, even though your wife won't be coming out for another month.

POKOV

But, sir....

KRUTZOFF

Pokov, I know what the regulations are, but I think I can make this decision without checking with Moscow, if that's all right with you.

POKOV

(Demurely, looking down, allowing his brief sneer to be seen by ILLUVYCH) I anticipated the general's good judgment and have already had the major's things brought to the married officers' quarters.

The silence is short, but uncomfortable. ILLU-VYCH salutes and leaves, closing the door behind him.

KRUTZOFF

(Furious; venting some of the anger) Look, Pokov, I didn't ask for this assignment. I know you think you should be sitting here, and I wish you were. (Reflecting) I will be out of your hair as quickly as I can, but I have to be sure that my enemies no longer fear me before I retire to some "quaint little *dacha*" out of harm's way. Until then, we're stuck with each other. (He touches the stars on his lapel.) I didn't get these for putting up with insolence. Just so we understand each other.

KRUTZOFF has made his point; POKOV nods quickly, with a degree more of humility. He walks over to the general and crisply opens the file, turns it around and hands it to the general.

POKOV

Sir, Moscow suggests that there could be an attempt to breach security at the test tomorrow night.

KRUTZOFF

(Visibly bothered) Any details? Who? How

many? From where? How?

POKOV

An American operation, sir. No details.

KRUTZOFF

Well, see to it, Pokov, won't you? The usual doubling of the guards, surprise inspection, that sort of thing. You know what to do better than me.

POKOV

Yes, sir. (He remains standing there, waiting.)

KRUTZOFF

Yes, (With annoyance) What else is there to be dealt with?

POKOV

Oh, I have nothing else sir. Do you have anything else for me?

KRUTZOFF

(Looking down, shaking his head) No, that will be all.

POKOV

Thank you, sir.

POKOV bows, snapping his heels together with deference, turns and leaves.

KRUTZOFF watches him leave. He has heard something he hadn't thought he would hear; could it be that POKOV would back off? He looks down at his papers, then looks up, and then POV out the window at the MiG-23 being pulled into the hangar.

As the camera tightens on the fuselage, the shot shifts to

SCENE VII - the fuselage of KAL 007 at its gate at Kennedy Airport.

SCENE VIII - Inside at the gangway, a stewardess is patiently waiting as the CONGRESSMAN is giving final instructions to his ASSISTANT.

CONGRESSMAN

Well then, Fred, you write to each and every one of them and you tell them that I will never compromise my position on this matter. The Communists have behaved themselves lately to lull some of the people at the White House into believing that they are really interested in peace. The only peace they know is better red than dead.

THEY are moving down the gangway to the door of the plane.

CONGRESSMAN (cont)

And I am not going to let the country go Communist because of petty politics. I will take care of it when I get back, and I'm sure they can wait until Monday. The Korean ceremonies are on Saturday, that's their time, so I'll be leaving Friday night our time, and getting back Sunday. That means I'll see you in the office bright and early at seven on Monday.

ASSISTANT

Sir, don't you think you'll want to take a day or two off to rest? I mean with the jet lag, and everything.

CONGRESSMAN

Thanks for the thought, Fred, but there's so much to do, there's no time to rest. No rest for the weary, HaHa. Anyway, I'll grab a nap on the plane.

They shake hands, and the ASSISTANT watches as the CONGRESSMAN turns and greets the stewardesses with Southern charm and

SCENE IX - is ushered to his seat. Before he can sit down, the CONGRESSMAN is recognized and is shaking hands with an elderly woman across the aisle. As he sits down, the camera focuses past the CONGRESSMAN several rows and finds Benton JENNINGS looking over the top of a magazine. The shot changes from the magazine

SCENE X - to a Playboy magazine. It is being admired by the CAPTAIN, sitting in the Pentagon Communications Command Center.

CAPTAIN

I don't know, Colonel, I think they should have given it to Miss June. She had something, you know, she was different. She had real allure.

The camera moves around from the CAPTAIN's face to see the LT. COLONEL standing at a data printer. He speaks without looking up from the console.

LT. COLONEL

Allure! You just like blondes with large boo---breasts.

The CAPTAIN sniggers, closes the magazine, and stands up. He stretches and then walks by the global satellite image, stopping in front of the panel that shows the area north of Japan. A dotted white line is looping from Anchorage to Hokkaido. As the line slowly increases dot by dot, a star with the numbers "RC-235H" moves with it.

CAPTAIN

Well, the board's quiet tonight, again.

There is a hint of disappointment in his voice, enough to cause the LT. COLONEL to turn to look at the CAPTAIN for a moment before turning back to his console.

The camera moves in on the lights and loses focus.

SCENE XI - The focus comes back on a chandelier; the camera is pulling back to the interior of an elegant Washington party. One conversation comes through distinctly, and soon the camera pulls back to find Norbert FOUNTS talking comfortably with Ed REIMER.

FOUNTS

I think we can let him cool out a bit. I mean the Premier has backed up so far, even Thatcher is worried that they'll fall off the edge of the Earth.

REIMER chuckles and clinks his champagne glass with his colleague.

REIMER

You're right, of course, and I think the timing will be perfect for the primaries. All we have to do is give 'em more space, with a couple of gentle growls now and then. They understand what elections are about. I think they'll cooperate.

FOUNTS

Let's have State leak to the French that we are willing to hold up production of half of the Pershings and see who screams when it gets out.

REIMER

I don't think we'll have any problem on the Hill. The Far Right is doing a free fall according to the latest polls. We'll look great in Minnesota.

THEY laugh together. They are joined by their WIVES, and the camera rack-focuses to the band, and quickly on a beat point, there is a musical transition

SCENE XII - to Prokofiev's *Lieutenant Kije* playing on the stereo in CHANEY's nesty living room. She has three pennies, paper and pencil, and the *I Ching* on a table next to her. She is eating from a cup of yogurt. She glances at the clock next to her with some concern on her face.

SCENE XIII - The scene changes from the yogurt to a greasy paper bag at the Pentagon. The CAPTAIN is taking food out and putting it on the desk. For himself, he has some KFC fried chicken; for the COLONEL, he has food from Burger King. The COLONEL walks over, puts money on the desk and picks up his Whopper, fries, and a shake.

LT. COLONEL

How can you eat that greasy crap?

The CAPTAIN makes NOISES behind his mouth filled with the chicken. He shrugs with a greasy smile. The COLONEL goes back to his console.

SCENE XIV - In the Sakhalin Command Center, General KRUTZOFF and Colonel POKOV are watching a wall of monitors from the back of the room, as preparations for the missile test continue.

POKOV points to a particular screen which, looking a lot like its Pentagon counterpart, is a map of the region, showing air traffic.

POKOV

You can see there, General, the American RC-235 is the red line, and the green one is the Korean flight from New York to Seoul. The Americans should be turning soon; it's a nightly run for them.

THEY watch as the two lines near each other, then the screen blanks, and a pulsating yellow warning light flashes. The screen blanks again for a moment, and then the lines are restored. The red line of the RC-235 is arcing away and the green line is continuing on its path. POKOV picks up a phone and asks some questions, waits, speaks again, and replaces the phone.

POKOV

(Angrily) The Americans have nothing better to do than to play jokes. They know our vectoring position, so they fly directly in front of the Koreans to confuse our radar. (Smugly) But as soon as they are a thousand yards apart, the computer can tell which plane is which.

KRUTZOFF

(Not as convinced, aware that POKOV is watching him; thoughtfully) Put up half of the new squadron. I want visual confirmation.

POKOV is about to question the order, but his hesitation is momentary. He picks up the phone again and issues an order, listens, speaks briefly and hangs up.

POKOV

We'll be up in a few minutes. It's hard to imagine that they would try anything around here, even using the Korean puppets. Particularly since there is a heavy ceiling at two thousand feet.

Even though they are in a windowless room, KRUTZOFF looks up, as though to better understand what is happening in the skies.

SCENE XV - MARGE and DAVID are looking at the sky as they walk, hand in hand, by the water's edge. The phosphorescence on the sand is like the starry night.

MARGE

It's taken you three days, but you certainly seem to have gotten your mind away from Washington.

STONE

(Smiling) It's funny how you can get so wrapped up in something, that you can't even see that you're in the middle of it.

HE puts his arm around HER, stops, and kisses her passionately on the lips.

STONE

We need to set up a secret code so that anytime I get in so deep that I can't see, you can say this phrase, and I won't be allowed to argue.

MARGE

Good idea. How 'bout I say, "David, darling, it's the job or me"? No, that might not get through. (Laughing; then in a deep, sexy voice) "David, it's time to get away, just the two of us."

STONE

(Somewhat taken aback by her sensuality) Uh, no. Let's find something else. I'd like to hear that one more often.

THEY both laugh and continue walking.

STONE

(Softly) You know, it's times like this that I think about kids. It's funny because I love you so much, and don't want to share you, but I just feel so good.

MARGE

I suppose that's what it's all about. Nurtur-
ing.

STONE

I wish I had more faith in the way we're
dealing with the Russians. We just seem to
be too close to pushing the button. I would
like to think that our children would have
a future.

MARGE nods; she's heard it before and doesn't
want to discuss it. She feels the conflict, too.

MARGE

(Sighs) We better be turning around soon if
we're going to get back in time for *Night-
line*.

STONE

(Pulling her closer) I think Ted can get by
without us tonight. That is, unless you're
dying to get back in front of the tube.

MARGE just smiles and pulls him closer as the
walk continues.

SCENE XVI - Major ILLUVYCH is sitting in the cockpit of his fighter, waiting to take off. He is re-reading a letter he was writing to his wife when his unit was scrambled. His letter is heard as the camera follows the take-off procedure.

ILLUVYCH

(voice over) *Maya dyevushka.* I arrived today in the middle of nowhere. Anywhere without you is nowhere, but this place is so bleak, I wonder whether you should follow me or stay in Tbilisi with your parents for a few months. You know how much I miss you, so you can imagine what it must be like here. I can't believe I was holding you only this morning; it seems years ago.

The MiG takes off.

SCENE XVII - The shot changes into the engine blast of an inboard engine of the KAL jet. The camera moves inside to the first-class cabin where the CONGRESSMAN is lecturing his cabin mates on the insidious nature of the Communist conspiracy in the Third World. While a retired couple is avidly soaking it up, most are merely paying polite attention.

Benton JENNINGS walks behind the group, pauses briefly to take it all in, then climbs the stairs to the lounge. He takes in the new scene – a couple of businessmen working out of their briefcases, and two newlyweds cooing in a corner. Behind the bar is the STEWARDESS. JENNINGS walks up to her with a smile. She reaches for a glass.

STEWARDESS

What can I get you, sir?

JENNINGS pulls out a leather ID holder and opens it in front of his chest, out of sight of the other passengers who aren't looking anyway.

JENNINGS

Please let me into the cockpit.

The STEWARDESS hesitates, and then nods, turning to the cockpit door. She takes out a small key, inserts it in the lock and turns it, knocking quietly as she opens the door. JENNINGS follows her into the cockpit, and hands the PILOT a letter. The PILOT reads it and then nods to the STEW-ARDESS to leave. When she has left, the PILOT gestures to a jump seat behind the co-pilot's position. JENNINGS smiles and graciously accepts.

PILOT

Certainly impressive credentials, Mr. ah, Davis, a letter from the head of military intelligence of the Republic of Korea ordering full cooperation. What can we do for you?

JENNINGS

(With a smile of control for the CREW around him) Gentlemen, we're going to fly a little off course tonight.

SCENE XVIII - At Sakhalin, KRUTZOFF is edgy but not panicked. The radar insists that the spy plane has turned around. The MiGs appear on the screen and intersect with the Korean flight. On the squawk box, Major ILLUVYCH identifies it as the Korean plane. KRUTZOFF is about to order them back, but looks questioningly at POKOV, who obviously wants to say something.

POKOV

General, their course has them intercepting our air defense perimeter in another forty-five minutes. The fighters are already up, why don't we leave them there for a while?

Moscow is very interested in our security status for this test.

POKOV has kept his voice even, inoffensive. The GENERAL nods his agreement. POKOV leans towards the console microphone, presses a button.

SCENE XIX - The scene changes to ILLUVYCH's cockpit, hearing POKOV's voice.

POKOV

Major, this is Colonel Pokov. We acknowledge your transmission. We would like to stay upstairs for a while.

ILLUVYCH's face registers disdain.

ILLUVYCH

Confirming, Colonel. (Waiting for his VOICE to be under control) Is there anything in particular we are looking for?

KRUTZOFF is privately pleased to see POKOV's face tighten.

POKOV

No, Major, we will tell you what you need

to know.

SCENE XX - In the cockpit of the Korean airliner, the NAVIGATOR informs the PILOT that they are ten minutes from the normal course correction. The PILOT looks up at JENNINGS, who says nothing, stares ahead into the moonlit void. The CREW exchange glances among themselves.

SCENE XXI - The shot changes to the party, and REIMER and FOUNTS exchanging glances of false pleasure as they are listening to their HOSTESS extol their power.

HOSTESS

It just seems like the president is always on vacation, which is good for a man his age. Oh. (Putting her finger delicately to her lips) I mean, there is so much to remember. (The two AIDES raise their eyebrows and nod agreement.) He must really trust you to take care of things when he is away. But I'm sure the government is in good hands with you two .(TITTERS) I just feel so honored that you could take time away from those Russians, and the Jews and the Arabs, and those welfare people, to spend time relax-

ing. You know, with the people who understand and appreciate what a great job you are doing. And it is such a pleasure that you people are in office. I mean, the previous administration, well, I heard it told that they would have world leaders to eat at the White House, and guess, just guess what they would serve them? (SEES the helpless shrugs) I know you're not going to believe me, but (HOLDS two fingers up in an old Brownie's salute) I swear they served those world leaders fried chicken.

SCENE XXII - The camera pulls back from the CAPTAIN's chicken bones making a big greasy spot on the bag they came in.

CAPTAIN

Looks like those Korean cowboys are at it again.

LT. COLONEL

(Coming over to join the CAPTAIN at the map) Are those fools pushing the border again tonight? (Annoyed rather than concerned) You'd think they'd get bored.

The next blip of the KAL plane illuminates inside a thin, red perimeter line marking Soviet airspace.

SCENE XIII - The screen changes and it is a similar set up in the Sakhalin command center.

KRUTZOFF

(Concerned) Dammit. Those fools would pick tonight to play games.

POKOV

(Excited) Do you think this is what the alert could be about?

KRUTZOFF

(The thought had occurred to him and he had rejected it. Now he was reconsidering. His voice is hard, not betraying the worry.) Tell the wing to escort the plane out of our territory.

POKOV speaks into the microphone. As his order is given, ILLUVYCH banks his plane into position in front of the KAL jet.

SCENE XXIV - In the cockpit of the KAL airliner.

PILOT

(Looking at the NAVIGATOR) How far in are we?

NAVIGATOR

Seventy-five miles already. And on this course, only another hundred miles from Sakhalin. (For JENNINGS' benefit) Our maps show that as very sensitive, Captain.

JENNINGS remains impassive, checking his watch with deliberate slowness and looking out at the MiGs.

PILOT

Mr. Davis, I'm not questioning your authority, but we've got 269 people on this plane who were planning to get off the plane in Seoul in a couple of hours.

JENNINGS merely nods. The PILOT looks at the NAVIGATOR, who urges him to push harder.

PILOT

Mr. Davis? We've been known to skirt the border before, a couple times a month, just to keep the Russians on their toes. But not this far.

POV - Two MiGs suddenly flash across in front of the plane.

JENNINGS

Calm down, Captain. You don't question my authorization, do you?

PILOT

(Backing down somewhat) No. But at least tell us what we're doing.

JENNINGS

(To the NAVIGATOR) Stay on the current heading for another ten minutes, and then make direct for Seoul.

NAVIGATOR

(Poring over his charts; then very concerned) But that will take us to within fifteen miles of Sakhalin Base.

JENNINGS says nothing.

CO-PILOT

(With a finger on his headphones) Captain, Tokyo is asking why we are off course.

JENNINGS

(To the PILOT) Tell them that your equipment says you are on course, that you will check again and get back to them. Also tell them that they are coming in very scratchy.

The PILOT nods at the CO-PILOT, who repeats the information into the headset.

SCENE XXV - The camera pulls back from the cockpit into the cockpit of ILLUVYCH's MiG. (Back and forth conversation)

ILLUVYCH

They have to see us, Colonel. We passed a hundred yards in front of his nose.

KRUTZOFF

Have you tried to contact him by radio?

ILLUVYCH

Yes, sir, and through visual signals.

KRUTZOFF

And no response?

ILLUVYCH

No, sir. Nothing.

POKOV

General, they are only sixty miles away. If they stay on course, they are going to be within ten miles of the base when the test goes off.

KRUTZOFF

What do you suggest, Pokov? (In an attempt to calm them both)

POKOV

(Cautiously, within his rights) Perhaps we ought to contact Central, sir.

KRUTZOFF peers at his subordinate, weighing the military and political decisions. He takes a key from his pocket, inserts it into a small lock on the console, and pulling it open, takes out a red, dial-less phone. He picks up the receiver, turns his back on POKOV, and carries on a brief conversation. He turns back to POKOV.

KRUTZOFF

(With dismay and controlled alarm) They were having a private party and wanted to know if it was really something that I couldn't take care of myself. (He replaces the phone; resigned) Remember, Pokov, power is a double-edged sword.

POKOV stands waiting, disconcerted, but action-oriented.

KRUTZOFF

Order the major to fire warning shots in front of the cockpit.

SCENE XXVI - The view is from the cockpit of the Korean airliner: explosions light up the sky. The terror is palpable. In the cabins, squeals of glee from the children who think they're watching fireworks, but near-panic among the adults. The CONGRESSMAN is obviously concerned, but he advises his fellow passengers to remain calm.

As a third and fourth round explode in front of them, the cockpit door opens and the STEWARD-ESS steps in. Startled, JENNINGS spins around with an automatic in his hand and nearly fires.

JENNINGS

Get out! (He grabs her key, pushes her, and slams the cabin door. Then he turns to the crew.) Now we are going to do this as planned. In (HE consults his watch) four minutes, you'll be able to turn this ship around and we can all go home. You can say that you had a problem with the guidance system, and discovered it was caused by someone using a portable computer in the back of the coach cabin. (To them and to himself) There's nothing to worry about.

PILOT

Mr. Davis...

JENNINGS

No questions, Captain. (The gun is pointed loosely in his direction.) I'll tell you when to make the turn. (To the CO-PILOT) I'll take your headphones.

The CO-PILOT reluctantly hands them over. As JENNINGS puts them on, the NAVIGATOR lunges at him. JENNINGS steps back and hits him in the side of the head with the automatic. The man crumples to the cabin floor.

SCENE XXVII - The scene switches to the Pentagon

CAPTAIN

Colonel, there's something wrong here. That KAL flight is much too far in. Either the gear's on the blink (Tapping the side of the electronic map), or we've got a real problem.

LT. COLONEL

You've confirmed that it's the KAL; our man is out of the area.

CAPTAIN

Yessir. Checked it twice. Tokyo agrees. Says their last transmission said they were getting okay guidance readings and would check it out. They also said they were having some radio problems. (HE turns from the map to the LT. COLONEL.) The Russians must be having one big fit. (HE giggles .)

SCENE XXVIII - Back in the Sakhalin Command Center.

POKOV

Sir, you've got to do something. They will be over the test area in less than five minutes.

KRUTZOFF

Pokov, I appreciate your interest in the security of the test, but I'm not sure it is a very good idea to shoot down a civilian airliner that may simply have strayed off course.

POKOV

Sir, we use civilian aircraft all the time. It is merely a matter of mounting an infrared camera and taking long range pictures of the firing.

KRUTZOFF

Through a cloud cover?

POKOV

(Shrugs, nervous) We don't know their exact technology, General. We don't even know if that's the real Korean airliner; it could be a fake.

(He calls to ILLUVYCH for confirmation.)

ILLUVYCH

Colonel, if it's a fake, they found a lot of people to go along with it.

POKOV

(Growing desperately excited) Sir, this could be what Central alerted us against. They could be testing you!

KRUTZOFF feels attacked, and suddenly very uncertain.

KRUTZOFF

Pokov, make up your mind. Who's flying that plane up there, Moscow or Washington? (He leans over the console and presses the microphone button.) Major, can you suggest some way to prevent that airliner from flying over this position? Other than, of course, destroying it.

ILLUVYCH

No, general, I can't. We tried everything I was taught. We have even had visual contact with the pilot.

KRUTZOFF

Try again. And if he doesn't respond in the next sixty seconds, shoot him down.

ILLUVYCH

(Disbelieving silence) General, that's a civilian airliner, you can't...

KRUTZOFF

(With fury) You are a major, and I am a general! (Pauses; calmly) We have reason to believe that it is not what it appears.

ILLUVYCH

Sir, I can see women and children moving in the plane.

KRUTZOFF

(Icily) Then I suggest you try very hard to convince the pilot to change his course in the next thirty seconds.

SCENE XXIX - In the cockpit of the KAL airliner, JENNINGS studies his watch intently and then pushes a button on the side of it.

JENNINGS

Ready to start your turn, Captain. In five seconds, four, three, two, one.

The PILOT throttles back and puts the giant plane in a hard turn.

JENNINGS

(Handing the headphones back to the co-pilot) You can tell Tokyo that you have discovered your guidance system error and are correcting your position for a direct to Seoul. You expect to clear Russian airspace in three minutes. Tell them you've still got radio problems and you would advise their continued monitoring. (LAUGHS with relief) Come on, Captain, you didn't think the Russians were going to shoot down a civilian airliner, did you?

The NAVIGATOR stirs on the floor of the cabin. JENNINGS helps him into his seat and speaks to him gently.

JENNINGS

It's all right, son; it's all over, we're heading home.

SCENE XXX - In the Pentagon, the CAPTAIN utters an audible sigh.

CAPTAIN

I guess the Koreans decided that one 747

didn't need to tangle with those eight buzzards, huh, Colonel. They just up and turned your basic one-eighty.

LT. COLONEL

(Muttering) The fools. One day the Russians are going to live up to their reputation for paranoia and blow a plane right out of the sky. They sure are going to make a lot of noise about this one.

SCENE XXXI - In the Command Room, ILLU-VYCH's voice comes over the squawk box.

ILLUVYCH

(With relief) They've turned around, General. (KRUTZOFF feels POKOV's stinging glance) They're on a direct route for the edge of our airspace.

POKOV

(Sarcastically) Thank you, major. We'll call you when we lose our radar.

A phone on the board rings. POKOV listens briefly

and then hangs up.

POKOV

We intercepted a transmission from the plane. They said their guidance system malfunctioned and they were adjusting course. They also continue to say they are having trouble with their radio.

KRUTZOFF

(Willing to share his gratitude with his subordinate) I'm glad we didn't shoot them down, then, aren't you, Colonel?

POKOV

(Not so sure) It could be a trick, you know, General. It's the easiest excuse in the world.

KRUTZOFF

(With generous patience) Still, I'm glad we didn't have to shoot it down.

SCENE XXXI - On the plane, people are settling

back into their seats. The PILOT announces that there had been a minor course error that had been corrected, and that they expected to be landing only ten minutes late in Seoul. The CONGRESS-MAN is gesturing that there never was anything to worry about.

On the flight deck, JENNINGS pushes another button on his watch.

SCENE XXXII - At the Sakhalin Command Center, the phone rings, and POKOV picks it up. Suddenly he is very animated. He holds the phone away.

POKOV

General, communications is picking up garbled radio transmissions from the jet-liner. They say they haven't seen the pattern before. It must be some new kind of code.

KRUTZOFF

(Taking the phone) Who do they seem to be sending to? Is there any acknowledgment? (Listens) What do you think it could be? (Hangs up.) (To POKOV) The signals are going to Hokkaido, but they don't know of a base there and there's been no acknowledgment. (POKOV waits) They say the signals could be encoded video signals.

POKOV

(Nearly frantic, as he peers at the radar screen, and then back at the general) General, they will be out of our airspace in forty-five seconds. If they were taking pictures – I don't know how! – and were transmitting them to the ground....

KRUTZOFF

(Pushing the microphone button) Major Illuvych, fire one more warning shot in front of the cockpit, and if they don't respond, shoot them down.

ILLUVYCH

But General, they've turned around, they're leaving.

KRUTZOFF

Fifteen seconds, major.

SCENE XXXIII - In the plane, the atmosphere is looser until suddenly another shell bursts in front of them.

PILOT

What the hell are they doing? We're going already.

JENNINGS face shows alarm; he knows they discovered his transmission.

JENNINGS

(To the navigator, a tremor in his voice) How long until we're out of their airspace?

NAVIGATOR

(After a moment) We should be clear in five seconds.

SCENE XXXIV - In the cockpit of the MiG , beads of sweat are on the major's brow as he flicks switches on his control panel and positions his plane behind the KAL airliner. On his windshield is projected the ghostly outline of the 747 with the engines highlighted by target outlines. (Back and forth conversation)

KRUTZOFF

Illuvych?

ILLUVYCH

Nothing, sir?

KRUTZOFF

Then shoot. Now.

ILLUVYCH waits a fraction of a second and then pushes a button on his console. A wisp of white smoke trails forward from under his right wing. It displays on the windshield as a red line. When it connects with the target, they both disappear from the screen. POV off to the right of his cockpit, ILLUVYCH can see the light of the explosion. The 747 is suddenly in front of him, without lights or power, electrical flashes coming from under what remains of the left wing. The plane is going down.

ILLUVYCH

(Lifelessly reports) Target destroyed.

SCENE XXXV - Inside the plane, the CONGRESS-MAN, his voice tremulous with terror, is reciting the Lord's prayer. In the cockpit, the CO-PILOT is frantically radioing Tokyo while the PILOT attempts to gain control of the plane. JENNINGS' face is frozen in shock.

SCENE XXXVI- The plane tumbles towards the sea, ILLUVYCH following it down. He watches as the PILOT vainly attempts to pull up the nose at the last moment, but the plane won't respond. The right wing catches the top of a wave and slams the plane to the surface of the water where it disintegrates.

SCENE XXXVII - There is SILENCE in the Sakhalin Command Center as they follow the blip of the 747 from the screen. (Back and forth conversation)

KRUTZOFF

(Into the console) Maintain your position, major, we're sending out naval units.

ILLUVYCH

(With anger and incredulity in his voice) No one survived, General. They hit the surface at over one hundred fifty miles an hour.

KRUTZOFF

Thank you, Major. If it's all right with you, we will attempt to recover the flight re-corder. And anything else that might be useful.

ILLUVYCH

Acknowledge, General. Will maintain my position.

SCENE XXXVII - At the Pentagon, the CAPTAIN and the LT. COLONEL stand looking at each for a moment.

CAPTAIN

Colonel, Tokyo confirms that KAL is off their screen. Sir, they say it was shot down.

Stunned, the LT. COLONEL picks up a special phone. He speaks briefly and hangs up.

LT. COLONEL

This is out of our league, Captain. The big
boys will be down to take over. Let's get
this place cleaned up.

HE crumples his food in their wrappers and puts
the mess in a trashcan.

SCENE XXXVIII - An elegant dessert is sitting half-
finished on the plate before Norbert FOUNTS. He
has a smile on his face, held in place by will, not
pleasure. The HOSTESS' voice is droning on about
the honor of having such important people grace
their presence. The phone rings in the hall. A
butler comes in and whispers something to the
HOSTESS.

HOSTESS

Perhaps their work is too important for him
to have a complete evening with us. Mr.
Founts, sir, you are wanted on the phone.

FOUNTS graciously leaves the room. There is a
strange look of jealousy and curiosity on REI-
MER's face. He looks up as FOUNTS is momen-
tarily back in the room, his face trying not to show
shock, obviously needing for them to leave.

FOUNTS

(To the HOSTESS, lightly) I am so sorry, my dear. Affairs of state and all that nonsense.

He signals REIMER, and then goes to his wife, whispers something to her and leaves.

SCENE XXXIX - CHANEY is doing the dishes in her kitchen the next morning, while she watches a cooking show on a small television next to the sink. She looks out the window above the sink, watching the steady rain. Suddenly the program is interrupted by a news bulletin.

SCENE XL - POV television

TELEVISION COMMENTATOR

The Secretary of State has an announcement regarding the missing Korean Airliner.

(CHANEY freezes) Ladies and Gentlemen, the Secretary of State.

As the voice of the Secretary of STATE fumes at the Soviets for shooting down the plane, the camera watches CHANEY. Her face expresses disbelief, fear, and pain. The sound of the STATE Secretary continues as she moves around the apartment. She goes to the pantry, takes down an unopened box of flour, rips open the box and takes out a plastic-wrapped revolver. Next she goes to the bedroom, lifts up a portion of the carpet, removes a floorboard, and takes out a small leather document case. Then she goes to the hall closet and pulls down hiking and camping gear.

The STATE Secretary's voice is cut off.

SCENE XLI - CHANEY comes out of her house and the front door closes. She gets into her car and drives off, looking around carefully. After a few blocks, she turns into a gas station, parking near a phone booth. She makes a call, hangs up and waits. In less than a minute the phone rings, she picks it up speaks only a few words, hangs up and returns to her car.

She drives to JENNINGS's house and disappears inside. Soon, she comes out into the garage with more camping gear. She struggles to open the trunk of JENNINGS' car. She transfers the camping gear from her car to his, and then drives off, leaving her car on the street.

SCENE XLII - Talking to the PRESIDENT by phone are FOUNTS and REIMER.

FOUNTS

We still don't understand why they did it,
sir, and they're not talking. None of it
makes sense.

REIMER

But we have it confirmed by the Soviet
pilot's transmission recorded in Tokyo that
he shot down the plane. That's why we
unleashed the Secretary this morning.
(Listens) Thank you sir, we were sure you'd
agree.

FOUNTS

(Listens) Yes sir, we will keep you up-to-
date as we get more information. (Listens)
No, we don't think it's necessary for you to
come back right away. At least not until we
know what happened. (HE looks over at
REIMER who nods agreement.) We are
preparing a statement deploring the situation, the mindless loss of life, et cetera.

REIMER

(Listens) Yes, Mr. President. Very strange.
And you're right, very ironic about the

Congressman. (Listens) They're planning some kind of vigil or service next week. (Listens) I don't think they've thought about it yet (Checking a file folder) but the likely bet is that his wife will get his House seat, probably until the end of term.

THEY both listen for a while, then promise to keep him informed, and hang up.

REIMER

I wish this made more sense, Bert, but I think you're right, we have no choice but to jump up and down and make a lot of noise, at least until we can find out what happened. And the Navy is doing all they can to get to the crash site, but the Russians are already there. So we will just have to wait and see what develops.

FOUNTS

The part I don't understand is why they haven't said anything. (Shaking his head) I am glad that all we're doing for the time being is making noise.

SCENE XLIII - CHANEY drives past a sign that

says Shenandoah National Park. She pulls into a nearly-deserted parking lot and parks next to a maroon BMW. She gets out, opens the trunk of JENNINGS' car and begins to unload the hiking gear. The MAN who had been sitting in the BMW gets out and helps her to load the gear into the trunk of his car. THEY work in silence, finish quickly, and get into the BMW. As the doors close, HE starts the car.

CHANEY

Why did we shoot it down?

SCENE XLIV - FOUNTS and REIMER are standing in an office, watching the afternoon news bulletin.

TELEVISION COMMENTATOR

Still no word from the Soviet Union on their downing of the Korean Airlines jet with 269 people on board. Reaction from around the world continues to pour in. A special session of the Security Council has been called....

REIMER

I still don't understand what they are waiting for. They can't stonewall it forever; not with all those people dead.

TELEVISION COMMENTATOR

...and a high administration official says that there is no excuse for shooting down the airliner, but they continue to await a formal explanation from Moscow.

FOUNTS

I'd take informal.

The phone rings. REIMER picks it up and listens.

REIMER

And? (Listens) Well, find him. I don't care if you have to use the Hundred-and-First Airborne, find that sonovabitch and bring him here. They're not dropping names for their health. (He hangs up; to himself but aloud) I don't think...? (To FOUNTS) A high-verification indication, that's Langley's term for a call from the KGB, says we should ask Benton Jennings about the crash.

FOUNTS

(remembering, with surprise) You mean that guy who ran the Border States campaign. I thought we stuck him somewhere safe.

REIMER

So did I.

FOUNTS

Do you think – pardon the expression – that it's a red herring?

REIMER

They don't think so over in Langley.

SCENE XLV - It's the next day, and DAVID and MARGE STONE are sitting at breakfast watching the morning news. STONE is clearly caught by his desire to cover the news, but also by his desire to escape its pull. MARGE is aware of his dilemma, sympathetic but standing back. On the screen, a picture of CHANEY appears behind the commentator's head.

TELEVISION COMMENTATOR

...and the FBI refuses to confirm that they are searching for Washington model Constance Chaney in connection with the official.

STONE drops his glass, it shatters on the floor.

MARGE

David? David, what's wrong? Did you know her? (Then she remembers something.) Isn't that...? Didn't you go out with her?

STONE

Yes, eons ago. This thing has gotten out of hand. I've got to make a call. He leaves the room and then returns with his address book. He dials her Washington number. For a moment, he is surprised when the phone is answered.

STONE

(He adjusts his voice) So, hey, I'm looking for Connie. (Listens) Just a friend, man, I didn't know...

He cuts off the call in mid-sentence with his finger

on the button. (Annoyed with himself for not expecting the strange voice) He looks in his address book again, finds another listing in Paris, with lines drawn through it. He calls the number. It's picked up on the first ring, and he recognizes a VOICE he hasn't heard in ten years.

STONE

Chaney, it's David.

There is a silence, and then her VOICE comes through distinctly.

CHANEY

(Hear her voice) David, I need your help. Can you come here? Now?

STONE

(Stunned; stammers) I'll be there as soon as I can.

The connection is terminated. HE looks at the phone a moment, then places it gingerly in the cradle.

STONE

(To his wife watching him from the kitchen) Darling, I have to go to Paris. I don't know what it's about... (He dials another number in his address book.) Hi, this is David Stone. I need to be in Paris as soon as possible. (Listens) No; business, unfortunately. (Listens and checks his watch) That'll be fine. No, an open return. Thanks.

SCENE XLVI - Back in Washington, FOUNTS and REIMER have just watched the broadcast.

REIMER

Since Hoover died, that place leaks like a sieve. Have they managed to find out anything more on either Jennings or the girl?

FOUNTS

Nothing on Jennings. The FBI says they have known about the girl for five months; the CIA is saying six months. But neither must have been paying much attention because she can't be found either. You know already that her car was parked in front of Jennings' place, and his car was up at Shenandoah. And there's a report that she might have gotten out last night. But nothing confirmed.

REIMER

Are we sure they're not pulling our chain with this thing about Jennings?

FOUNTS

No, but I sure would like to talk to the dumb sonovabitch myself.

The phone on the desk BUZZES. FOUNTS answers it, listens, says something and hangs up, looking expectantly at the door. It opens, and a SECRE-TARY walks in and hands him a manila envelope. Suppressing his temptation, he walks back to his desk and slowly undoes the flap with a letter opener. Inside are two sheets of paper, the passenger and crew manifest for KAL 007. One name, Harrison Davis, is circled.

FOUNTS shows it to REIMER, pointing to a small initial on the back of the envelope.

REIMER

(Whistles softly) So Langley says that Jennings was on the plane. Uh-oh.

FOUNTS

I think it's time to bring the President back. (He picks up the phone.)

SCENE XLVII - STONE is in an airliner on final approach to Charles De Gaulle Airport, but his mind is recalling the conversation he had with his wife before leaving. Their VOICES are first heard over his looking out the window at Paris at dusk.

STONE

I don't know really how to say it, honey; I don't have a handle on it yet. She said she needed my help. She knows the FBI is looking for her, and after ten years of nothing more than exchanging Christmas cards, she asks me to come to Paris.

MARGE

Exactly. And I want to know why. And why you're going.

STONE

Darling, please...

SCENE XLVIII - The shot changes to their kitchen and the actual conversation:

MARGE

I'm sorry, David. I understand, at some level. Part of me understands. I love you, and I guess I just haven't grown up enough not to worry about losing you. (Starts crying)

STONE

(Screws up his face in regret.) I will always come back to you, Marge. (Pauses) When we first met, I warned you that a journalist has a sense of his craft like a musician. Except the musician can bubble with energy when a new song comes to him. A journalist can feel something like that when he smells a story. This is a big story, probably the biggest I've ever known. Please give me the freedom to cover it without worrying about you. It hurts me to think that I am causing you pain.

MARGE

(Sniffles) I'm sorry, David, you're right. This is something that I have to manage by myself. It's not fair to you.

SCENE XLIX - STONE is jolted back to the present as the plane touches down and then taxis to and parks at the gate. He is carrying a shoulder bag, and quickly moves through customs. As he reaches the taxi stand, CHANEY – wearing a blond wig and low heels – takes his arm and propels him to the crosswalk to the parking garage. They walk two flights of stairs without speaking, STONE doing his part to maintain the masquerade by looking slightly tired and disinterested. They reach the top of a flight of stairs and step out into the parking area. Suddenly CHANEY stops, and pulls STONE back into the stairwell. She pulls off her dark glasses and the wig, tears are streaming down her face.

CHANEY

Oh, David, thank God you came. I could think of no one on the Earth to talk with, and then you called.

STONE

(Clearly not having known what to expect,
but somehow feeling surer at being there.)
It will be all right, Chaney.

SHE collapses against his chest, sobbing.

SCENE L - The sound blends into waves lapping
against the side of a Soviet destroyer (in the Sea of
Japan). A two-man submarine is being lowered
over the side.

SCENE LI - (On a television screen)

TELEVISION COMMENTATOR

As world condemnation of the shooting
down of Korean Airlines Flight 007, almost
as loud is the silence from the Soviet Union,
American naval vessels are steaming to the
crash site, hoping to find remains of the
plane, and particularly the flight recorder.

The camera pulls away from the monitor to see
FOUNTS and REIMER briefing the President.

REIMER

We wouldn't have asked you to cut short your vacation if we didn't think your presence was necessary, sir.

FOUNTS

The problem, Mr. President, is that we don't know what happened, yet...

PRESIDENT

Other than that the Russians shot down an unarmed civilian airliner with 269 people on board. That part seems pretty clear. What is it that you don't understand?

REIMER

Sir, we think that one of the people from Langley might have somehow been involved.

PRESIDENT

(Shocked) Who? How?

REIMER

The "who" is a man named Benton Jennings; he ran the Border States campaign for us. Nice guy, a bit stuffy, but reasonable.

PRESIDENT

(Sarcastically) And what did this nice man do that has the whole world in an uproar?

FOUNTS

We're not sure about that yet, Mr. President. But we think he might have done something, or else that the Russians have something they can say about him. That's why we think they haven't responded yet, officially.

PRESIDENT

(Watching REIMER pacing) So when do we find out?

REIMER

We felt that the situation was getting enough publicity that it would look better with you being at the helm and all. (Letting it sink in) And we'd also like you to talk to the nation on Monday night.

PRESIDENT

Saying what, that we think the CIA did it, but we don't know how or why?

REIMER

(Patiently) We're having something written now. It says how much we deplore such terrible behavior, and the issue of freedom of the skies, that sort of thing.

PRESIDENT

What else? (Suddenly concerned) Not another grain embargo? We'll lose the Midwest next year.

FOUNTS

Ah, no, sir. No embargo. No action, really. Just deep concern.

PRESIDENT

No action?

REIMER

That's right, sir. We feel it would be better to wait until we know the whole story before we *do* anything.

PRESIDENT

But this is so outrageous! No one should be shooting down civilian airliners. They're not armed. They're not spy planes. (Stops; sees his aides exchange glances) Are they?

REIMER

(Sighs deeply; after a pause) Probably. (He watches the PRESIDENT put his hands on his hips.) Most KAL flights are equipped with surveillance gear. Usually they aren't near anyplace that it's worthwhile. This time they happened to be only a few miles from Sakhalin Island at the moment of a thought-to-be secret test of a new SS-30.

PRESIDENT

And what part did we have in this insanity?
What did Jennings do?

REIMER

That's the part we're trying to find out sir.
The Russians let us know about Jennings in
the first place. He was supposed to have
been off backpacking with his girlfriend
(He looks at FOUNTS), but it seems he was
actually on the flight, using an alias.

PRESIDENT

Good grief! What about the girlfriend?
(Sees their hesitation.) Come on, enough is
enough, I want the whole truth.

FOUNTS

(Not wanting to say) It seems that she was
in the employ of the Russians.

PRESIDENT

(His mouth falls open.) You're not joking,
are you? (Looks at their silent faces.) Don't
take this personally, but I gotta tell you

guys, I sometimes wonder whether I've done the right thing by letting you run this place. When the whole story comes out, there's gonna be a lot of egg on a lot of faces. (Muses to back his threat) I want to know everything – (With sudden vehemence) every sordid rotten petty little detail – as soon as the information is available. (Heading to the door) Keep in mind what I have said, and let me see a draft of the speech this afternoon.

The PRESIDENT walks out, closing the door behind him firmly.

SCENE LII - The door to CHANEY's apartment building opens, and she leads STONE up a dark narrow flight of stairs to the second landing. CHANEY is talking as they climb the stairs.

CHANEY

So not having any idea what happened, but knowing somehow that Ben was dead, and knowing that I would be connected with him, I decided to call it all quits.

SCENE LIII - SHE opens the door to her apartment, and walks in with STONE behind her, closing the door.

STONE

Why did you take his car with all the gear up to Shenandoah?

CHANEY

(Uncomfortable) I didn't know what to do, but figured it could buy the time to find out...to get out. (Reconsidering) I don't suppose it was necessary, really.

STONE

So what do you do now that you are out of the spy business? Fourteen years in decadent Washington; aren't you going to miss any of that during the legendary frigid Moscow winters?

SHE looks at him with caring. His tone did little to disguise his feeling of regret for them, and his real caring. SHE takes his raincoat and hangs it in the closet. HE puts his bag down on a chair. SHE comes over to him and puts her arms around his neck. His hands move naturally to her hips.

CHANEY

(In a low voice, on the verge of breaking, but bolstered with integrity) It was never just a job, David. Ben and I loved each other. (More softly) Just as we did.

STONE stares into her endless grey eyes, looking for a reason to pull away. HER head moves slowly towards HIS, his moves towards her. Her lips reach for his mouth and press against it passionately. And quickly again, she draws back, keeping her hands behind his neck. STONE lets out a deep breath.

STONE

Well, I guess we know the answer to that part, don't we? (He undoes her hands and leads her to the sofa; struggling with himself) But that's not why I am here. (SHE nods. HE regains some of his composure) You couldn't have expected me to call. I shouldn't even have had your address, but I brought the wrong address book to the beach.

CHANEY

Synchronicity.

STONE

Oh come on, Chaney, not more of that Eastern psychobabble.

CHANEY

(Unable to stifle a laugh) Carl Jung is hardly a saffron-robed monk. (Laughs again) But you must admit that it's a pretty big coincidence. I mean, twelve hours ago, you were sitting on a North Carolina beach with your adoring wife, and now you're sitting in the Paris apartment of a Russian spy you used to date.

STONE

(Growls)

CHANEY

(Sliding closer to him on the couch) David, the best is yet to come.

STONE

I'm sorry to be difficult, Chaney, but I don't think we should go to bed... (She starts to interrupt) ...let me finish. (More gently) My heart and my body would like nothing more, even my "spiritual" side, as you call it, can't find a reason not to be tearing off our clothes right now. But...but I can't do anything that could hurt Marge. I know it sounds trite, but I'm not bright enough to handle it any better.

CHANEY

David, I would like to make love with you, and I will understand – (Smiling) sort of – if we don't. But that's not what I meant. (Sitting up straight) When you called, I saw a way *out* of possibly turning this into a more dangerous situation that sets back our efforts at cooling off our nuclear hostilities. (Somberly) Maybe Benton accomplished a lot more than he thought. (Getting up) Let me fix us something to drink and I'll explain.

CHANEY and STONE cross the living room, he settling onto a bar stool across the counter from her in the kitchen. She takes two glasses down from the cupboard, placing them on the counter in front of STONE, fills the ice bucket, and puts it down next to the glasses, and opens the liquor cabinet.

CHANEY

(Drawing out the bottle, smiling) Still Cutty Sark?

HE smiles back and nods. SHE places it on the counter in front of him, and goes back to the refrigerator, retrieving a platter of cheeses and pâtés. She takes a baguette from the bread box, and some small knives from a drawer and puts everything on the counter. Then she pulls a bottle of vodka out of the freezer, comes around and sits on another stool several feet away.

CHANEY

(Almost apologetically) You simply can't find this outside of Paris. I had to stop and pick this up on my way in from the airport yesterday.

SHE pours herself a drink.(Begins after a satisfying swallow)

Okay, you know the story of John Scali

acting as intermediary between your government and mine during the Cuban Missile Crisis. (STONE nods "of course") Because he was a respected journalist, and outside of government. He could not only pass critical information back and forth, but he was able to gauge feelings. He did a lot to help us through a couple of tense weeks.

Having a sense of what CHANEY is leading up to, STONE suddenly realizes that while he has no idea of the details of what is to happen, his instincts had been right about coming to Paris, and the dimensions of what he was dealing with.

CHANEY

There are some interesting parallels between then and now, in particular, that the Russians and the Americans are not talking directly to each other with any effectiveness, and it is more this lack of communication than what is being said that's causing all the concern.

SHE spreads some pâté on two pieces of bread, hands one to STONE.

CHANEY

When you called – not the details – but the general idea of using you.... (SHE hears herself; HE gives her a half-smile.) Sorry, David. ...the same way Scali was used popped into my head. As soon as I got off the phone, I checked with my superiors, and they agreed. They can't talk directly to the White House, and all other formal channels – ambassadors, Foreign Secretary, the United Nations – there's just too much mistrust, on both sides. But your people would have to listen to you.

STONE

(Allowing skepticism in his voice) And what would I say?

CHANEY

(Surprised and disappointed at his tone) Why, you tell them the information we are operating from, what we know, what we think happened, and that we want to clear this up.

STONE

(Caustically) It sounds so easy. Clear it up. They – you – shot down a civilian airliner with 269 civilians. (HER face falls. And HE realizes how much SHE feels the loss of their relationship; and that HE had been responding with jealousy; HE begins again gently) I'm sorry, Chaney. I was playing Devil's advocate. Even presuming that you can prove that Benton Jennings was in the cockpit, what did he do up there? Where's the proof that he was responsible for the flight path? Was he taking pictures of the new missile launch? And if he was, how could you prove it, or prove that he was transmitting them to some hidden secret base...

CHANEY

A weather base on a small island north of Hokkaido.

STONE

(Anger returning) You don't even know if the pictures could be taken through the cloud cover. And truly, most people aren't going to give a good goddamn if there were shots of Andropov in bed with some bimbo. You killed hundreds of innocent civilians, including many women and children.

CHANEY

(Quietly) David, I know that. We all do. Everyone is so uptight with all the rhetoric that we are losing sight of the key to the whole thing. Nothing was done in a vacuum. A general in Sakhalin who was worried about his retirement ordered the plane shot down. He didn't know for sure that if it wasn't some kind of trick. For fifty years, he's been living in his distrust of your people, and he made a mistake.

STONE

(Without anger, shaking his head) Some mistake.

CHANEY

Don't patronize me, David. We are talking about human beings, with all their frailties. He sees two blips on his radar screen, one he knows to be one of your RC-235s, the other supposedly a civilian airliner. It's

Korean, state-owned and run, staffed by ex-military or KCIA people. The plane ignores all signals, encroaches into top secret Russian airspace much further than any previous incursion, all of this – coincidentally – exactly the time of the testing of a secret new missile. Then they pick up coded – probably video – transmissions from the plane. They tried radio contact, fly-by's, warning shots, and nothing. They order the fighter to launch an R60 – what NATO refers to as an Aphid-A at the suspect aircraft. What would you have done? (HE opens his mouth) Don't bother. My point is that we have all these security systems in place. How far do you let yourself be pushed before you use them? What difference does it make what side he's on? (Thinks of Jennings; suddenly angry) You can play Devil's advocate for whoever you want, but don't feed me that sanctimonious nonsense about innocent civilians. Your policies in Central America are causing tens of thousands of innocent deaths.

CHANEY is breathing heavily when she finishes. SHE tries to hold back her tears, but they come anyway. SHE turns her head away, and does not see STONE slide off his stool. When SHE turns back, HE is standing in front of her. SHE throws her arms around him and sobs on his shoulder. HE holds her, squeezes her, and lets her cry.

STONE

(With a far-away look) This is a very strange time, isn't it?

SCENE LIV - A television newscast, showing pictures of protests around the world. The shot pulls back to show MARGE watching with conflicting feelings and a large drink. SHE [comments] on the script and the production.

TELEVISION COMMENTATOR

It is the silence by the Russians that is the most incendiary fuel for this firestorm of public opinion. More pieces of wreckage – and of human remains – have washed up on the beaches of islands in northern Japan. [Jesus!] But as yet, the black box – the flight recorder which could reveal the possible reasons for the Korean pilot to have lost his way – has not been located. [Lost his way!?] The search for that black box over the suspected crash site is a tense one, with American, Russian and Japanese vessels all operating in the same area. One report said that a Russian ship and an American destroyer came within shooting distance – sorry, that's shouting distance – [Idiot!] of each other. At the United Nations, the incident prompted the American ambassador to warn the Soviet ambassador not to cause any more casualties than they already have. And here in Washington, the Pentagon has ordered a nuclear carrier task force to sail for the site of the salvage operation. The task force, based in the Philippines, will be in position in three days.

MARGE

In position for what, you idiot. (Gets up, spills her drink) Damn! (SHE snaps off the television; looks longingly out the window) Oh, David, please come home soon.

SCENE LV - STONE and CHANEY are sitting at a small table in front of a bay window in her flat overlooking the city.

STONE

Okay, I think you're right, I can get in to see Reimer. I can tell him everything (Looking at her) – *everything* (She nods) – that you've told me. But it's still only circumstantial evidence.

CHANEY

Until we find the black box.

STONE

If anyone finds the black box. And even then, we don't know what, if anything, will be on it.

CHANEY

(Trying a new tack) David, my government has been trying to get better relations with Washington and the rest of the world. We're not trying to take over the world. We are not going to bury you; that's a lot of old Cold War talk. We've got the same problems domestically that you do, and we would like to spend our resources dealing with them. As you would. But it's going to take time. The premier is not going to stand in front of the Washington Monument and proclaim that it's all been a game, that he wants Russia to be the 51st state.

STONE

It's true, he has been making a lot of concessions on the missiles in Europe.

CHANEY

Exactly.

STONE

That's why this whole thing didn't make any sense. You people seemed to be so much more conciliatory, then you shoot down the plane. It didn't fit.

CHANEY

(Firmly) No one has a good reason to shoot 269 civilians out of the air.

STONE

Chaney, how much authority are you operating with? I mean, they're going to ask that.

CHANEY

The highest. And they know your govern-

ment is going to be suspicious, so they want to prove their intentions are honorable.

SHE gets up, walks to the window sill where SHE takes a photograph from inside a book and brings it back, handing it to STONE.)

This is your top undercover operative in Moscow. He will have 48 hours to leave Moscow after you have been to the White House. If he goes quietly, we will say nothing.

STONE

(With raised eyebrows) Our – my government doesn't know that his cover has been blown? (SHE shakes her head) Did they know about you?

CHANEY

Yes, for about six months; that's why it was necessary to leave. Once they knew about Benton, they would have brought me in. Since I don't have diplomatic status, they would have thrown me in prison, or traded me back. There are no rules, but the play can get very dicey during a crisis.

STONE

(Gently) But Benton didn't know. (SHE shakes her head.)

HE sits looking out the window, absent-mindedly tapping the table with a pencil.

Okay, this is what I want to do. I want to tape an interview with you – your people, your equipment is fine – and you will tell me about your relationship with Jennings, what he said to you, what you did when you heard about the plane, and why.

CHANEY

(Weighs it; unperturbed but cautious) What else?

STONE

(Shrugs) That's it. The tape will give me the credentials to persuade my bureau chief to get me into the White House. The photograph will give me as much credibility – if you're sure they don't know that this guy's cover is blown (SHE nods) – as we can possibly have. Is there anything else you can tell me?

CHANEY

(Looking at him intently) My instructions are to give you whatever information you need to get them to understand. If we find what we think we will in the black box...

STONE

Presuming it's found.

CHANEY

(Nods) ...then the world will know that the U.S. provoked the crisis. (Holds up her hand to stop him from interrupting, her voice heating up) I know, I know, 269 is a statistic to you. Remember, one of them was a man I cared about. (Pauses to let it sink in for a moment; then conciliatory) Of course we shouldn't have shot down the plane. But we are damned lucky that, with fifty thousand nuclear warheads between us, larger mistakes haven't happened yet.

STONE

You know I understand all that. (Very gently, stroking her arm) I guess I just find it hard to take it all in, considering where we are now.

CHANEY

(Covering his hand with her own; very softly) I know, David, it's strange thinking that the planet could be at a crossroads, and you and I, where we were, could have a role in creating a future.

STONE

(Non-belligerently) More of that synchronicity stuff?

CHANEY

(Standing, moving towards the phone, stops, thoughtful, smiling) Maybe.

She picks up the phone, dials, hears a response and starts to speak.

SCENE LVI - The shot shifts to Dulles Airport. STONE is in a phone booth, his shoulder bag tucked under his arm.

STONE

It's David Stone. I need to see you right away. (Listens) Of course I know what time it is, Harry. (Twisting to see his watch, then seeing an electronic display which says that it's Tuesday at 2:14 in the morning) Where shall I meet you at three. (Listens) Yes, you hosted the Christmas party last year. Good, I'll be there in forty-five minutes. (Hangs up and re-dials) .

SCENE LVII - The shot changes to a phone ringing in the moonlit bedroom of the STONE's beach house. The sound jolts the body under the sheet. Suddenly, moving as if she'd been awake, MARGE picks up the phone.

MARGE

David, please say it's you.

STONE

(Eyes moisten) Yes, Marge it's me. Everything is okay. I just got into Washington and I wanted to tell you how much I love you.

MARGE

Oh, darling are you all right?

STONE

Yes, Marge. Fine. I can't talk about it now, but I'll tell you everything when I see you.

MARGE

Are you coming back down to the beach, or should I come back to Washington?

STONE

(Considers) I really want to be with you, but I have a sense that I'm going to be running for a while. It might be easier if you stayed there for another day or two. I'd love to get back there with you. We can unplug the phone and put the television in the closet. You've got another ten days before you have to get back.

MARGE

I miss you, David. I love you. Call me when you can. I'll leave the phone plugged in until I see you.

There is silence. Then MARGE hears the phone being placed in the receiver. She squeezes the phone to her cheek and then puts it back in the cradle. She rolls over, her smile illuminated by the moon shining through the window.

SCENE LVIII - The shot changes to the early morning sun in ED REIMER's office; the clock on his desk reads 6:44. STONE is with him.

REIMER

(Light, almost jocular) You must have told Harry Damon quite a story. He said I had to see you as soon as possible, and he would- n't tell me why. He has a substantial repu- tation in this town, and he put it on the line for you.

STONE

He did not compromise his reputation, Mr. Reimer, and I hear you. He saw a tape of an interview I did yesterday with Constance Chaney. (He has to cover a smile when REIMER's jaw drops.) But it's bigger than that.

HE takes the photograph out of his pocket and

hands it to REIMER. REIMER studies it without apparent recognition.

STONE

I am told that the Russians know this man to be our top undercover operative in their country. They said that if he leaves within 48 hours – from our meeting – that they won't say anything.

REIMER

(Almost dizzy; he pushes a button on the phone) Get me the duty officer at Langley. (Hangs up; trying to regain his composure) All right, presuming your credentials are in order, who gave you this information and why?

STONE

Chaney. Her government thinks this KAL incident has gotten out of hand because WE don't know what happened. (REIMER gives a snort) Their evidence, though circumstantial, indicates that a high-level CIA officer is responsible for provoking the Soviet attack.

REIMER

(Annoyed) We know all about Jennings being on the plane, Mr. Stone. And we have known for some time that Miss Chaney was working for the Russians.

STONE

Sir, it was the Russians who sent the passenger list to the CIA.

REIMER is watching his control slip away; he gets a break when the phone BUZZES. He picks it up, listens a moment, then pushes another button.

REIMER

Good morning, Commander. I need someone who knows the faces of our top operatives behind the Iron Curtain. I need that person in my office fifteen minutes ago. (Listens) Yes, I know what time it is, Commander, and perhaps that will make it easier to find someone before he leaves for the office. (Listens) Thank you. (Hangs up)

STONE

The Russians also provided the original information about Jennings. They want you to have the information they are working with. (REIMER harrumphs) Sir, if that is in fact a photograph of our top operative, that's a big gift. And with the leads they've given you already, you must consider the possibility that they genuinely want to resolve this situation.

REIMER

(Haughtily) You are telling me what I must consider, Mr. Stone? Perhaps you will explain to me why the Russians picked you to be the courier? It sounds like Scali in '62.

STONE

Circumstances.

REIMER

Don't play coy with me!

STONE

(Holding his temper) I am suggesting, Mr.

Reimer, that the Russian viewpoint is far more significant than my story. (More subdued, diplomatically) I am not hiding anything from you; I am simply aware of the value of your time. I will answer any questions, but please hear me out.

REIMER

(Stroked) All right, what did they say?

As STONE beings to tell the story, the shot moves to his notebook. Then the shot dissolves to the notebook, many pages deeper, showing he's finished his story. The shot is back in the room.

STONE

And, sir, if you would indulge another perspective ... (REIMER is obviously defenseless) ...I've been a journalist for fifteen years, and I have never seen the Russians behaving this reasonably. They could have gone public with this information, but instead, they are giving it to us.

REIMER

(Thinks) Is there anything else, Mr. Stone?

STONE

(Considers for a moment) No, sir. I think that's all of it. (Standing)

He shakes REIMER's offered hand.

REIMER

(Holding the photograph) I trust you don't mind my hanging onto this for a while.

STONE

No, sir.

REIMER

And you won't say anything about this man?

STONE

(Takes a deep breath) Not if he leaves Moscow within 48 hours.

REIMER

(Incredulous) Are you threatening me?

STONE

No, sir, I'm not. I certainly can't imagine any reason why you wouldn't take the Russians upon their generous offer. And if you don't, the Russians will either arrest him or throw him out. In which case, it will be a significant news story.

The phone on the desk BUZZES again. REIMER picks it up.

REIMER

(Into the phone) Send him in. (To STONE) Let's find out if it's an issue at all.

The door opens and a recently-asleep face on top of a stiff three-piece suit comes through the door.

REIMER

(Without any formalities) Do you know what our top operatives in the Soviet Union look like?

CIA DEPUTY

Yes, sir.

REIMER hands him the photograph. The MAN can't disguise his shock.

> REIMER
>
> I gather you recognize him.

> CIA DEPUTY
>
> Yes, sir.

> REIMER
>
> That big, huh.

> CIA MAN
>
> Yes, but how...

> REIMER
>
> Thank you, that will be all. Please use the phone in my outer office to call him. He has (Checking his watch) forty-seven hours to leave Moscow. Instruct him to do so. Good day.

The CIA DEPUTY leaves. REIMER looks out the window, suddenly vulnerable and sincere.

REIMER

Wouldn't it be nice if everyone stopped playing games? We waste so much time and energy.

STONE

(Surprised and grateful at the man's vulnerability) Yes, Ed.

REIMER

(Taken aback by STONE calling him by his first name, and by his capacity to be surprised he smiles) Thank you, uh...

STONE

David.

REIMER

Yes, sorry, David. I'm sure we can reach you through your office if the need arises.

STONE

(Nodding deferentially) They will know where I am. (Leaves)

REIMER picks up the phone, pushes a button.

REIMER

Communications, what transmissions did we pick up from the Korean plane in the last ten minutes before it went down. (Listens) No, not Tokyo control, probably a weather station to the north. (Listens) Well, check with Langley. Don't ask them "if", tell them we want it.

SCENE LIX - The shot changes to the white-capped foggy Sea of Japan. A squawk box on the deck of the Russian destroyer.

DIVER

We've got it! We're coming up.

The SOVIET COMMANDER hurries to the wheelhouse and picks up a microphone. He talks excitedly and then hurries back on deck. The crew moves to the side of the boat. Soon the mini-sub breaks the surface. The top hatch opens, revealing the two divers. They are smiling broadly. They hold up a net bag, and in it is the black box.

But before they can begin to climb up onto the

ship, there is a sound of helicopters, and out of the fog from different directions, six gunships with U.S. markings appear. They hover in a perimeter around the destroyer. The horn of a U.S. destroyer is soon heard and then seen knifing its way through the waves to within fifty yards of the Russian destroyer. The SOVIET COMMANDER can be seen shouting into the microphone. (Back and forth conversation)

US COMMANDER

(From the bridge) The divers will remain in the water. Do not attempt to change your position.

SOVIET COMMANDER

(Holding a telephone away from his mouth as he shouts back) We have no intention of moving from this spot. But we are in international waters.

US COMMANDER

We know where we are. We want the material your divers retrieved.

SOVIET COMMANDER

You must be familiar with the international laws regarding salvage operations, Captain.

US COMMANDER

Yes, Captain, as familiar as I am about the laws regarding the shooting down of an unarmed civilian airliner with an American Congressman on board. I am sure that you are aware of your position and our superior firepower.

SOVIET COMMANDER

(HE is; evenly) You will allow me the courtesy of contacting my government, won't you, Captain?

US COMMANDER

Of course, Captain. My government seeks to avoid violence...If possible.

While he is waiting, the US COMMANDER, responds to a voice in the wheel room, and ducks out of sight. He takes the phone angrily, but is suddenly and clearly stunned by what he hears.

US COMMANDER

(Incredulous) You want me to let a couple of commies on board our ship, sir? I mean, we could take the box and blow them right out of the water. (Listens) No, sir. (Listens) Yes, sir. (Listens) *Yes,* sir. (Listens) *Yes, sir.* Right away, sir. (Walking out onto the bridge; his tone substantially less belligerent) I am instructed that the black box will be delivered to us by your two divers.

SOVIET COMMANDER

(Speaks into his microphone) Accepted, captain. If you lower a boat for them, they will be glad to accompany their salvage back to Japan.

US COMMANDER

(To his EXEC) They keep changing the rules.

SCENE LX - The shot changes to Washington, and STONE emerging from the bathroom into the office of the Washington Bureau Chief.

STONE

My first trip to the executive washroom, Harry. It's all it was cracked up to be.

DAMON

(Grunts, picks of the phone in the middle of the first ring, hears the voice, and quickly sits up) Holy Ghost! (Listens) Yes, I'll tell New York. (Listens) Right. (Listens) Okay, right away. (Hangs up) That was the radio desk at the White House. They found the black box, the Russians did, and *we took it from them.* The stuff is on its way to Tokyo to be examined, with two Russians along. The President has announced a national speech at three, and they want to see you.

STONE

Who's they?

DAMON

Reimer.

STONE rubs his hair vigorously as he returns to the bathroom and closes the door.

SCENE LXI - The shot changes as the door to the Oval Office opens.

The PRESIDENT gestures to STONE to come in. REIMER, FOUNTS, the PRESS SECRETARY, and the President's VALET are with him.

PRESIDENT

Come in, Mr. Stone.

Standing, the PRESIDENT walks around the desk, offering his hand. He shakes STONE's and leads him across to two couches divided by a coffee table.

PRESIDENT

Sit down, we have some talking to do. Would you like something – coffee, a Bloody Mary, something to eat? I hear you-'ve been on the go.

STONE

Ah, thank you, yes sir, coffee would be great. (To the President's VALET) Black, thank you.

PRESIDENT

Now Mr. Stone, some people get intimidated by the office, this one (gesturing) or the one I hold. This being intimidated can get in the way of my finding out what's going on. But we can't have that now. The times call for more clarity in our communications. But (HE pauses while the VALET puts a cup of coffee in front of STONE, who mouths a "Thank you"), but I guess I don't have to tell *you* that, do I, Mr. Stone?

STONE is taking a sip; he burns his lip trying to answer. HE shakes his head.

PRESIDENT

You have a very good reputation in this town, maybe not as big as the high-priced talent, maybe you're a little young, but no one has journalism in their blood like you. That's what I've heard. (STONE's ears redden.) I'm sorry, Mr. Stone, I was just trying to tell you that I'm listening, real hard. And I'm also a lot smarter than some of your colleagues think, so just talk to me straight, the way you want, and I'll listen. I'll only interrupt you if I don't understand something. Okay?

STONE

(Takes a breath, is about to start, takes another breath) Thank you, sir. I appreciate your perspective. (Starting) I was asked, by whom I understand to be high Soviet officials, to present their view of the downing of the plane, and the information they are dealing with. I have been thoroughly convinced of their desire to find a solution to this problem, without further recriminations.

STONE recounts everything he has learned, delivered in key sentences, phrases, and names. During the course of his recital, there is a series of wide and tight listening shots of the PRESIDENT, FOUNTS and REIMER. All STONE leaves out is his past relationship with CHANEY. STONE's cup is refilled. And FOUNTS and REIMER watching, see the PRESIDENT becomes more serious, and more thoughtful.

STONE

That's about it. (He wants to say something else.)

PRESIDENT

Go ahead, Mr. Stone, I would be disappointed if you left this office thinking there
was something left unsaid on this matter.

STONE

Sir, until the shooting down of the plane, it
seemed like the Russians were trying very
hard not to provoke us. They didn't go into
Poland after all, and they seem to be extri-
cating themselves from Afghanistan. (With
a slight edge of concern) And, if what I
heard this morning is true, they didn't
make a big fuss about our taking the black
box from them. In fact, the Russians think
they have been demonstrating an historic
attitude of conciliation. They haven't un-
derstood our seeming unwillingness to
meet them part way. A lot of people in this
country – while trusting your leadership –
have also heard a difference in their tone.
Now, if they're right about what happened
on board the airliner, they're going to ex-
traordinary lengths not to use it against us.
As they might have. You must know that
the Premier is facing a lot of pressure to
take a tough stand with us. Is it possible,
that we could share the humility of this

experience, and use it in a positive way?

Before the PRESIDENT can answer, a SECRETARY comes in and whispers something to REIMER, who bends over and whispers it to the PRESIDENT.

PRESIDENT

Let's put it on the speaker phone. (REIMER looks questioningly.) Go ahead, Ed, we're all going to have heard it a dozen times by tomorrow. It's the destroyer. It turns out that the ship was equipped to handle the black box salvage operation. Electronic gear, and all. Hello, Commander.

US COMMANDER

Mr. President?

PRESIDENT

That's right, Commander. Were you able to get anything out of the black box?

US COMMANDER

(Proudly) Yes, sir. It's clear as day, but I'm not sure I understand it.

PRESIDENT

Can you play it for us? (Has an idea) No, wait. Commander, I want the Soviet premier to hear this at the same time I do. I presume they are able to monitor this transmission, but have your communications officer try patching through to the Kremlin. We'll call from this end and tell 'em what you're doing. (He nods to REIMER who picks up an extension.) (They sit quietly for an uncomfortable several minutes.) (To the whole room) You know, you never get so big that you don't have to wait. (Laughter)

PREMIER

Hello, Mr. President, can you hear me?

PRESIDENT

Yes, hello, Mr. Premier, (wryly) I can hear as clearly as if you were calling from your embassy here in Washington. (The PREMIER laughs.) Mr. Premier, I am sitting

here with Mr. David Stone. (Pauses THEY
hear talking among themselves at the other
end.)

PREMIER

Oh, yes, Mr. Stone, the television commentator.

STONE's ears redden again, and the President
winks at him.

PRESIDENT

That's right, if you're ready, Mr. Premier, I
will ask them to play the tape from the
black box.

PREMIER

We are ready, Mr. President

PRESIDENT

Okay, Commander. Go ahead.

US COMMANDER

Yes sir. The tape runs three minutes and has a lot of gaps in it. The last audio on the tape is the sound of the co-pilot telling Tokyo they have decompressed. The tape ran another minute and a half, but there was no other signal recorded. (Waits for a comment; there is none) Here it goes...

(Electronic hum)

JENNINGS' voice: Ready to start your turn, Captain. In ten seconds ...five , four, three, two, one.

Engine noise lessens.

JENNINGS' voice: You can tell Tokyo that you have discovered your guidance system error and are correcting your position for a direct to Seoul. You expect to clear Russian airspace in three minutes.

Tell them you've still got radio problems and you would advise their continued monitoring. (laughs) Come on, Captain, you didn't think the Russians were going to shoot down a civilian airliner, did you?

The MEN in the Oval Office exchange glances of disbelief.

JENNINGS' voice: It's all right, son; it's all over, we're heading home.

PILOT's voice: Ladies and Gentlemen, sorry for the fireworks. We have experienced a minor malfunction in the guidance system, which back-ups have now corrected. We are now on a direct course to Seoul, expecting confirmation from Tokyo on that in just a minute. Our course's variation took us a little close to the airspace claimed by the Soviet Union, which explains the fireworks from the Russians. But. we didn't go far, so we expect to arrive at the gate in Seoul no more than ten minutes late. Thank you.

TOKYO's voice: Confirming your new heading, KAL 007, tracking you at 254 degrees, that's west southwest on 254 degrees.

CO-PILOT's voice: Roger, Tokyo KAL 007 acknowledges heading 254. Thank you.

(Silence)

(Sound of shell burst)

PILOT's voice: What the hell are they doing? We're going already.

JENNINGS' voice: How long until we're
out of their airspace?

NAVIGATOR's voice: (After a moment) We
should be clear in five seconds.

(No conversation for a few seconds) (Explo-
sion/Shouts/Electrical crackling)

CO-PILOT's voice: Tokyo this is KAL 007,
we're going down, we're going down. No
power. No power. Losing compression...

PRESIDENT

(After nearly a minute of waiting, and
reflecting; quietly) Mr. Premier, do you
think you would be able to have a brief
conversation with me, in about fifteen
minutes?

PREMIER

(Solemnly) I will await your call, Mr. President.

SCENE LXII - STONE's interview with CHANEY is playing on television. The shot pulls back to reveal the small television on the counter in the kitchen of the Stone's beach house. MARGE is cooking bacon while watching the interview. Her eyes register her different interests. When the interview finishes, she changes channels.

TELEVISION COMMENTATOR

...speech to the world last night, the President announced that the Americans and the Russians would jointly share the responsibility for paying compensation to the families of the passengers on Korean Airlines Flight 007.

PRESIDENT

The Premier and I today pledged that this painful lesson shall not go unheeded. Ours is a world on the brink. The United States and the Soviet Union share the burden of responsibility for this situation, and the duty to turn us back from the edge. We do not operate in a vacuum, however. All nations of the world must understand the need for peaceful resolution of disputes. It has been said that war is in man's nature. It is not true, it cannot be true. And the first step to achieving peace, will be to believe that. The Premier...

The door to the bedroom opens, and soon STONE emerges from the hallway. He is wearing a bathing suit, his hair is mussed, his face still creased from the linen. He walks to the kitchen where MARGE, also in a bathing suit, has been making breakfast. SHE is holding a plate with his breakfast that she was going to bring into the bedroom. HE carefully puts his arms around her and presses his mouth to hers. SHE puts the plate on the counter behind her. SHE pulls back, trying to get her breath, and feigning shyness.

MARGE

My goodness, David, a night's sleep certainly did wonders for you. (Kisses him again)

STONE

(Between kisses) Was there some problem with last night? Did you not have a good time?

MARGE

(She manages, purring) David, it was marvelous.

STONE

Come on, let's get some of those morning beneficial sunshine rays. After all that time working when we should have been playing, I want to tan up.

MARGE

You're hardly pale, David. (SHE sees he's not changing his mind.) All right, I'll leave breakfast in the oven and we'll have it for brunch in an hour. How's that?

STONE

Good plan.

While SHE's wrapping the plates in aluminum foil, DAVID is mixing up a pitcher of Bloody Mary's. MARGE smiles when she sees what he's doing and gets some plastic glasses out of the cupboard.

SCENE LXIII - THEY walk out of the kitchen, grab towels off the deck railing, and walk over the dune to the beach. MARGE lays out the towels, puts the cups down into the sand between the towels. DAVID pours. They sip their drinks.

> MARGE

These are so good with the fresh horse-radish.

> STONE

(Agrees) Aren't they? Oops. We forgot to toast. You say.

> MARGE

Hmm. (She thinks) How 'bout to peace with the Russians?

STONE

That sounds like another good plan. (They gently touch their glasses together.) Clink.

MARGE

Remind me what you were explaining to me last night before...

STONE

Before you distracted me?

MARGE

You are such a revisionist, David Stone!

STONE

But you are not complaining.

MARGE

Not in this case. Okay, tell me.

STONE

(sighs) This was from a talk I delivered to

the Psychologists for Social Responsibility in New York a couple of years ago. It was about how our two countries were having trouble communicating because of our very different world views. For instance, we are Uncle Sam and they are Mother Russia, which reflects a more distant relationship between Americans and our government. Their symbol is the bear, a very grounded animal, while ours is the eagle, which flies free. And in global politics, what we and our European allies call containment, the Soviet Union views as encirclement.

MARGE

Aaarrggghhh! How do we ever work things out?

STONE

Yes, that's the problem. But we need to stop viewing it that way, that it's insurmountable, and instead see them as challenges. Our differences are cultural, but they don't have to make us enemies. We could let go of the pretense that we need 100,000 troops in Europe to protect it from the Soviets invading. It's phony. It's posturing. They would never invade Europe. Europe is by far their major trading power. Their economy would be destroyed, even if we didn't go to war over an invasion.

MARGE

So why don't we bring our troops home? It must be costing us a fortune.

STONE

It does. We spend over $100 billion on forces overseas. Neither the Democrats nor the Republicans have the courage to stand up for cutting the fat and corruption out of the military budget because they would be accused of undermining national security. Of course it wouldn't. It's nuts. Very expensive nuts.

MARGE

So we just wear ourselves down, we and the Russians, spending money that should go to needs at home, until...until when?

STONE

That's much of what history recorded.

(Pauses) But I think we will come through this, darling, and in our lifetimes. It's certainly possible that someone mad would get into office and decide to end it all. Or there could be a technical glitch. It just seems curious that you and I, and other good people – those we know and those we don't – would be here at this time and not have some significant role in building a bright, healthy, rewarding future. (Sighs) So if downing the Korean Airliner is where we started to make the turn, it will have been, amazingly I think, over an incident that cost only 269 lives. And that rogue CIA agent, albeit with very different intentions, will have put us on the road to peace.

MARGE

I like that. (She has been writing S-T-O-N-E in the hard wet sand with her toe.) I've marked it in stone.

About the Author

Tony Seton is a journalist, writer, and publisher. An Emmy award-winning broadcast journalist for ABC Television News, he covered Watergate, six elections, and five space shots. And he produced Dan Cordtz's business/economics coverage and Barbara Walters' news interviews.

Later, Tony wrote and produced two award-winning public television documentaries.

Through Seton Publishing, Tony has written, designed, and published more than 50 of his own books and screenplays, and has edited and published 30-some books for clients.

As a political consultant, his clients have included Nancy Pelosi, Tom Campbell, John Vasconcellos, the American Nurses Association, and various local candidates.

He has taught journalism and writing, provided media training, and produced websites.

Tony is also a private pilot and a photographer.

SETON
PUBLISHING

www.ingramcontent.com/pod-product-compliance
Lightning Source LLC
Chambersburg PA
CBHW071959170626
46813CB00005B/1937